Fall Weather Fun

Martha E. H. Rustad

Illustrated by Amanda Enright

LERNER PUBLICATIONS ◆ MINNEAPOLIS

NOTE TO EDUCATORS

Find text recall questions at the end of each chapter. Critical-thinking and text feature questions are available on page 23. These help young readers learn to think critically about the topic by using the text, text features, and illustrations.

Lerner Publications Company
A division of Lerner Publishing Group, Inc.
241 First Avenue North
Minneapolis, MN 55401 USA

For reading levels and more information, look up this title at www.lernerbooks.com.

The photos on page 22 are used with the permission of: Alexey Lysenko/Shutterstock.com (leaves); Evgeny Atamanenko/Shutterstock.com (rain); Pressmaster/Shutterstock.com (snow).

Main body text set in Billy Infant 22/28.
Typeface provided by SparkyType.

Library of Congress Cataloging-in-Publication Data

Names: Rustad, Martha E. H. (Martha Elizabeth Hillman), 1975- author. | Enright, Amanda, illustrator.
Title: Fall weather fun / Martha E. H. Rustad ; illustrated by Amanda Enright.
Description: Minneapolis : Lerner Publications, [2018] | Series: Fall fun (Early bird stories) | Audience: Ages 5-8. | Audience: K to grade 3. | Includes bibliographical references and index.
Identifiers: LCCN 2017061719 (print) | LCCN 2017053539 (ebook) | ISBN 9781541524941 (eb pdf) | ISBN 9781541520059 (lb : alk. paper) | ISBN 9781541527225 (pb : alk. paper)
Subjects: LCSH: Autumn—Juvenile literature. | Weather—Juvenile literature.
Classification: LCC QB637.7 (print) | LCC QB637.7 .R86825 2018 (ebook) | DDC 508.2—dc23

LC record available at https://lccn.loc.gov/2017061719

Manufactured in the United States of America
1-44341-34587-12/19/2017

TABLE OF CONTENTS

Whoosh!
Wind blows colorful leaves across
the yard.
Fall weather is here.

We grab our jackets
when we go outside.
The air feels cool.

Today our class celebrates the first day of fall.
People call this day the fall equinox.

On the equinox, day and night are the same length.

During fall, each day is a little shorter than the day before.

Every morning, the sun rises later.
Every night, the sun sets earlier.

What is the first day of fall called?

CHAPTER 2
CHANGING WEATHER

In fall, the weather changes from warm to cold.

Fall weather feels cooler than summer weather.

Fall weather feels warmer than winter weather.

Fall weather changes from day to day.
We check the weather each morning
to decide what to wear.

In September, we wear light jackets. By November, we might need warm coats and mittens!

How does the weather change in fall?

CHAPTER 3

WEATHER CHART

Our class is making a weather chart this fall.

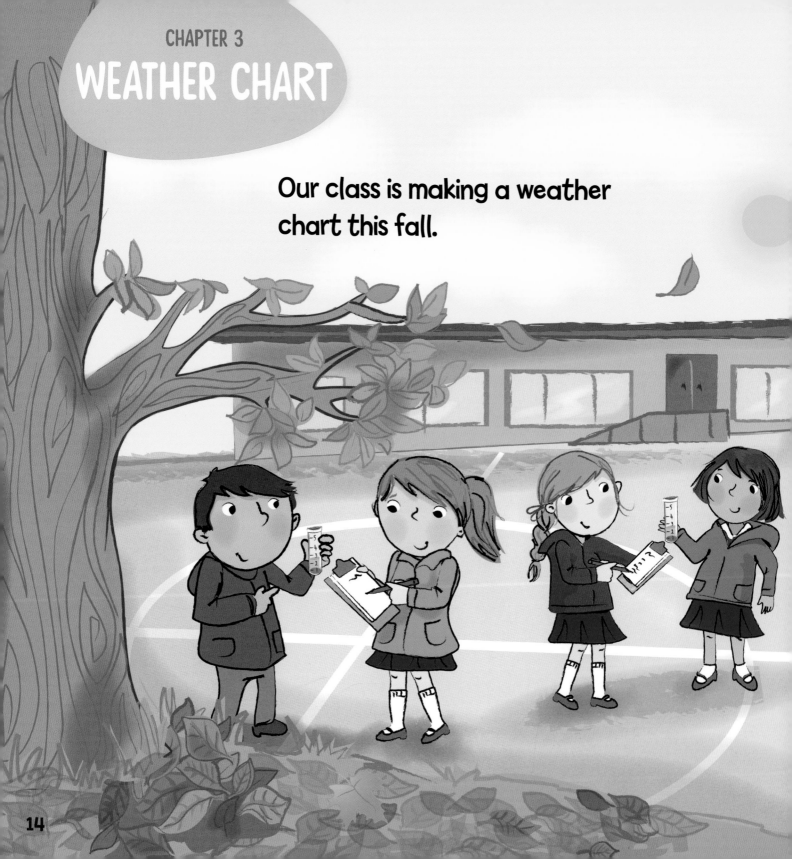

Every day, we write down how much rain fell.

day	date	rain gauge	temp
Monday	11/2	2.5 in. (6 cm)	50°F (10°C)
Tuesday	11/3	1 in. (3 cm)	48°F (9°C)
Wednesday	11/4	3 in. (8 cm)	39°F (4°C)
Thursday	11/5	0 in. (0 cm)	43°F (6°C)
Friday	11/6	0 in. (0 cm)	35°F (2°C)
Monday	11/9	1 in. (3 cm)	34°F (1°C)
	11/10	1 in. (3 cm)	34°F (1°C)

We write down the temperature too.

Some days, we write down warm temperatures.
Some days, we write down cool temperatures.

We notice that the temperature is going down.

We compare our chart with charts
from classes in other places.

One class has warmer weather.

Another class has more rain.

My class has snow in the fall.

Fall weather is different
from place to place.

Is fall weather the
same in every place
in the world?

CHAPTER 4
FALL ENDS

Fall is nearly over.
We wear heavy coats to stay warm outside.

Soon snowflakes fly
through the air.
Winter is almost here.

How does the
weather change at
the end of fall?

LEARN ABOUT FALL

Fall and autumn are names for the same season. People call the season fall because leaves fall from trees during this time of year.

The word *equinox* means "equal night."

Fall ends on December 21 or 22. We call the first day of winter the winter solstice. It is the shortest day and longest night of the year.

Some parts of Earth do not have fall weather. Near the middle of Earth, the weather stays the same all year.

Some places have a rainy season during fall. People in these places carry an umbrella or wear a rain jacket nearly every day.

THINK ABOUT FALL:
CRITICAL-THINKING AND TEXT FEATURE QUESTIONS

What is fall weather like where you live?

Why do you think the weather might turn cooler when the days get shorter?

Can you find the warmest temperature on the chart on page 15?

Which chapter in this book is about the end of fall? How do you know?

LERNER
e
SOURCE™

Expand learning beyond the printed book. Download free, complementary educational resources for this book from our website, www.lernerresource.com.

GLOSSARY

chart: a sheet giving information organized in lists or boxes

equinox: the date when day and night are each twelve hours long. The spring equinox is March 19, 20, or 21, and the fall equinox is September 22, 23, or 24.

temperature: how hot or cold something is

TO LEARN MORE

BOOKS
Felix, Rebecca. *How's the Weather in Fall?* Ann Arbor, MI: Cherry Lake, 2013. Find out more about how the weather changes in fall.

Schuh, Mari. *I Feel Fall Weather*. Minneapolis: Lerner Publications, 2017. Read more about wind, rain, and cool temperatures.

WEBSITE
Activity Village: Autumn
https://www.activityvillage.co.uk/autumn
Celebrate fall weather with games, puzzles, and crafts.

INDEX